Ballpark Mysteries 3

THE L.A.
DODGER

THE L.A.
DODGER

by David A. Kelly
illustrated by Mark Meyers

A STEPPING STONE BOOK™
Random House 🏠 New York

This book is dedicated to my editor, Jennifer Arena, who knows the secrets of good mysteries and takes the mystery out of good writing.
—D.A.K.

To Grandma K, thanks for always having your door open!
—M.M.

"I say this from the bottom of my heart, that if you don't root for the Dodgers, you might not get into Heaven."
—Tommy Lasorda, Los Angeles Dodgers Manager

Text copyright © 2011 by David A. Kelly
Cover art and interior illustrations copyright © 2011 by Mark Meyers

Visit us on the Web!
SteppingStonesBooks.com
www.randomhouse.com/kids

Educators and librarians, for a variety of teaching tools, visit us at
www.randomhouse.com/teachers

Library of Congress Cataloging-in-Publication Data
Kelly, David A. (David Andrew)
The L.A. Dodger / by David A. Kelly ; illustrated by Mark Meyers. — 1st ed.
p. cm. — (Ballpark mysteries ; 3)
"A Stepping Stone Book."
Summary: Cousins Kate and Mike visit Kate's father, a baseball scout for the Dodgers, in Los Angeles just as a series of suspicious events lead him to think that someone is trying to steal his scouting reports.
ISBN 978-0-375-86885-6 (pbk.) — ISBN 978-0-375-96885-3 (lib. bdg.) —
ISBN 978-0-375-89968-3 (ebook)
[1. Baseball—Fiction. 2. Stealing—Fiction. 3. Cousins—Fiction. 4. Dodger Stadium (Los Angeles, Calif.)—Fiction. 5. Los Angeles (Calif.)—Fiction. 6. Mystery and detective stories.] I. Meyers, Mark, ill. II. Title.
PZ7.K2936Lad 2011 [Fic]—dc22 2010038728

Printed in the United States of America
10 9 8 7 6 5 4 3 2 1

Contents

Spotting
Movie Stars

Mike Walsh leaned over to look down the aisle of the airplane. Good. No one was coming. He unbuckled his seat belt and stepped into the aisle.

"Watch this," Mike said to his cousin Kate Hopkins. She was in the seat next to his. It was spring break, and Mike and Kate were flying by themselves from New York to Los Angeles to visit Kate's father. He worked as a baseball scout for the L.A. Dodgers.

Mike jumped up as high as he could. His fingers reached for the ceiling.

THUD. When his feet hit the floor, his knees buckled. He steadied himself and then dropped back into his seat.

"Oh brother," Kate said, rolling her eyes. Mike wasn't afraid to try silly things. She thumbed through a shopping catalog that she had found at her seat. It was filled with baseball jerseys for dogs, self-inflating seat cushions, bug vacuums, and other funny things.

"I don't get it. The pilot said we were going five hundred and thirty miles per hour," Mike said as he buckled his seat belt. "I thought I'd fly to the back of the plane if I jumped up. That would be soooo cool!"

Kate shook her head. Her dark brown ponytail wagged back and forth. "And soooo not possible," she said. "You're going five hundred and thirty miles per hour, too, even when you jump. It's no different than jumping on the ground."

"You kids okay?" asked Rich, one of the flight attendants. Kate's mom had asked him to keep an eye on them during the flight. "Did you need help getting something, Mike?"

Mike blushed. "No, thanks," he said. "I was just stretching."

"Good idea! It's a long flight," Rich said. "Let me know if you want anything."

Kate put away the catalog. Then she fished around in the seat pocket in front of her. She pulled out a blue L.A. Dodgers notebook and a book with a photo of the big white Hollywood sign on the cover.

"What's that?" Mike asked.

"It's a guidebook to Los Angeles," Kate said.

"My mom gave it to me for the trip." Kate's mother worked as a reporter for the American Sportz website. Her mother and father had divorced when Kate was two. She lived with her mother in Cooperstown, New York, just down the street from Mike and two blocks away from the Baseball Hall of Fame. Mike's mom and Kate's mom were sisters, so Kate and Mike were cousins. They were also best friends.

Kate leafed through the book. She wrote down the sights she wanted to see in the Dodgers notebook.

Bored, Mike flipped down the tray table from the seat in front of him. He grabbed a book about the Los Angeles Dodgers from his backpack and started reading.

"Hey, did you know that the Dodgers did this, too?" Mike asked.

Kate stopped writing. "Did what?" she asked.

"Tried to jump up and touch the ceiling?"

"No, not that. The Dodgers flew to L.A. from New York, just like us. They used to be the Brooklyn Dodgers from New York City," Mike said. "They moved to L.A. in the 1950s. It says in this book that a lot of the fans in Brooklyn were really upset. They wanted the Dodgers to stay in Brooklyn."

"Hopefully they're over it by now," Kate said. "New York still has the Mets and the Yankees. That's pretty good."

"Yeah, but people in Brooklyn really loved the Dodgers," Mike said. "Their name is even connected to Brooklyn." He held out the book for Kate to see one of the pictures. "Back when the team first started playing, there were lots of trolley cars in Brooklyn. People had to *dodge* them to cross the street. So they called the team the Dodgers!"

"Well, my dad says the main thing you have to watch out for in L.A. is traffic," Kate said. "So maybe they should change their name to the L.A. Traffic!"

Mike groaned at Kate's joke and went back to his book. The rest of the flight was smooth, and the plane landed in L.A. around five o'clock. When Rich led them to the baggage claim area, Kate spotted her father right away. Mr. Hopkins was wearing a bright blue Dodgers warm-up jacket, a white shirt, jeans, and cowboy boots. Kate ran over and gave him a huge hug.

"*Hola!*" Kate said. *Hola* meant *hello* in Spanish. Kate liked to practice Spanish with her dad. Mr. Hopkins had spent several months traveling in Mexico and spoke it with ballplayers. Sometimes he sent Kate emails in Spanish for her to translate.

She stepped back and looked at her dad's shiny black leather boots. They had a fancy white design carved into them. "Nice boots!"

"Thanks," he said. "I bought them when I was in Arizona for spring training. They seemed fun." Mr. Hopkins leaned over and gave Mike a hug. "I'm glad you could make it out here, Mike. Haven't seen you since last summer. It will be nice to take the week off from work. It's been . . ."

Kate's dad paused for a moment as if he had forgotten a word. His jaw clenched up. He tugged aside his jacket and pulled a small black notebook out of his shirt pocket. He looked at it and slid it back without even opening it. He shook his head slightly and smiled. "Things have been a little crazy lately," he went on. "But that's not your problem. We're going to have a fun week."

Kate held up her blue L.A. Dodgers notebook. "Well, I wrote down all the things *I* want to see while we're here. *That* should keep us busy."

A loud buzzer went off. It was the signal that the luggage had arrived. Soon, suitcases of all colors were dropping one after the other onto the baggage claim carousel. Mike and Kate dashed over to wait for their bags.

"Is your dad okay?" Mike whispered to Kate. "He seems a little tense."

"Yeah, you're right. It's probably just his job or something," Kate said. "I'll bet having us here will be good. Maybe he can help us look for movie stars. The guidebook says you really *can* see movie stars around L.A."

Kate and Mike scanned the airport for celebrities. Mike pointed to a woman wearing

a red dress with a white bow. "Think she's a movie star?" he asked.

"She looks a little like Colleen Baxter from that TV show," Kate said, "but she's older. What about him?" She pointed to a squat little man in a white shirt and sunglasses. He wore a blue baseball hat with an old-fashioned *B* on it.

"I don't know," Mike said. "With that hat, he looks more like a Boston Red Sox fan than a movie star. What about that woman near your father?" He pointed to a tall lady wearing a stylish hat and carrying a blue bag.

Kate squinted and shook her head. "That could be the woman from that vampire movie," she said. "But I don't think it is. I guess it's not our lucky day."

Behind them, more suitcases crashed onto the baggage claim belt.

"Ooh, there's mine!" Mike shouted. A dark suitcase with baseballs along the edges fell on top of a red suitcase. "And there's yours! At least our bags made it. I think that's pretty lucky."

Mike and Kate scrambled to grab their suitcases as they moved past. Mike plucked his off the belt first. When Kate bent down to grab her suitcase, her backpack swung off her shoulder. She had to drop everything to snag her suitcase before it passed by.

"See, it *is* our lucky day," Mike said. "You almost missed it."

Kate gathered the rest of her things, and they headed back to her father. He led them out to the car and stowed the bags in the trunk. Mike and Kate hopped into the backseat. "Anything you want to see on the way to my apartment?" Mr. Hopkins asked as he buckled his seat belt. "It's about thirty minutes to Santa Monica."

"Let me look at my list," Kate said.

She rummaged through her backpack for a moment and then looked up at her father. "Wait!" she said. "My notebook is missing!"

Fortune Cookie
Warning

"I know I didn't put it in the trunk with the suitcases," her father said. "Are you sure it's not in your backpack?"

Kate took another look. While she did, her father opened up his jacket again. He checked the small notebook in his shirt pocket. He seemed lost in thought for a moment.

"No, it's not here," Kate said. "I definitely had it just before we got our suitcases, because I showed it to Mike."

Mike snapped his fingers. "That's it!" he said. "Suitcases! I'll bet you left it by the baggage claim. Remember when your backpack slipped off? You put your backpack and notebook down. Maybe you didn't pick it up again."

Kate unbuckled her seat belt, opened the door, and hopped out. "We'll be right back, Dad," she said.

Mike and Kate ran inside the airport to the luggage area. It had emptied out. Only a few unclaimed bags were left. Kate stopped at the spot where she had pulled her suitcase off the carousel. There was no sign of the missing notebook.

Kate searched the area. She even peeked under the edge of the carousel. Mike checked the seats and nearby hallways.

"I asked the janitor about it," Mike said

when he returned to Kate. "He just cleaned here. If the notebook were here, he would have found it. That means someone must have taken it!"

Kate frowned. "Drat. I knew I should have put it away! Well, at least there wasn't anything special in there. Just the list of things I wanted to see in L.A. Okay, let's go back to the car."

The ride to Mr. Hopkins's apartment was pretty quick. He lived in a tall building on Ocean Avenue. It was across the street from Pacific Palisades Park and the ocean. After unpacking, Mike, Kate, and Kate's dad walked a few blocks to a Chinese restaurant on Wilshire Boulevard. The restaurant wasn't crowded. They sat at a round booth in the corner.

"So, Mike, I know you're a baseball expert," Mr. Hopkins said after they had ordered. "Can you tell me what's unusual about Dodger Stadium?"

"Um . . . let's see." Mike leaned back in his seat and thought hard. "Oh, I know!" he said, snapping his fingers. "Dodger Dogs!"

Mr. Hopkins chuckled. "Good guess. I know that most fans think the Dodgers' hot dogs are special, but I was thinking of something else. Something about the park itself."

Mike thought some more. Finally, he shrugged. "I give up. What?" he asked.

"The dugouts!" Mr. Hopkins said. He took a pen from his shirt pocket and drew the outline of a ballpark on a white paper napkin. "Usually the home team's dugout is along the first-base line. But in Dodger Stadium, the visiting team sits on the first-base side. The home team is on the third-base side. Any idea why?"

"So the Dodgers can get to the hot dog stand faster?" Mike asked.

"No, not even close." Mr. Hopkins laughed. "Think about something big and bright and hot."

"The sun!" Kate blurted out.

"Exactly," Mr. Hopkins said. "The team put the home dugout there so that the sun wouldn't shine directly into the players' eyes during afternoon games. Instead, the visiting team sits in the sun, while the Dodgers stay cool in the shade."

"That's mean," Kate said. "You're supposed to treat your guests nicely."

"Not in baseball," Mr. Hopkins said with a smile. "The visiting team often gets a smaller locker room or older showers. Some clubs even cut the grass to different heights to throw the other team off. It's fair to do anything within the rules to give your team an advantage."

Mr. Hopkins slid the pen back into his shirt pocket. As he did, the smile left his face. He seemed deep in thought again as he checked for the small black notebook. Then he glanced nervously around the restaurant.

"Dad? You okay?" Kate asked. "You've been acting weird since you picked us up."

"I'm sorry," he said. "Work has been a little tough lately. But I'm trying not to think about it."

"Is something wrong?" Kate asked.

Her dad sighed. "Over the past month, strange things have been happening to me and other Dodger employees. Someone stole a few of my old scouting reports. My car was broken into two weeks ago. And sometimes I feel as if I'm being followed," he said. "At first I thought I was just imagining it. But last week, I heard that a few items, like notebooks, had been taken from coaches and managers."

Kate touched her father's arm. "Sorry, Dad," she said. Then she pointed to his shirt pocket. "Are you worried about that notebook? You keep checking it."

"Those are my scouting notes. They're

very important. If someone takes them, they'll know which players we're tracking," Mr. Hopkins said. "I'm going to give them to my boss after the game this week."

"Why don't you type the notes into your

computer and email them to your boss?" Mike asked. "Wouldn't that be safer?"

"Our email system has been broken into," Mr. Hopkins said. "My boss doesn't want us sending anything important that way. Also, my laptop computer was stolen last week. Luckily, I had already deleted my scouting reports. I copied them into this notebook instead. I haven't let it out of my sight since."

"This is pretty creepy," Kate said. She scrunched over, closer to her father. "Are we in danger?"

"I don't think so, or I wouldn't have let you come," Mr. Hopkins said. He put his arm around Kate and gave her a hug. "I'm not sure who's causing all this trouble or what they want, but we should be fine."

Their talk was cut short when the waiter came back with their meals. Kate devoured her beef with broccoli, while Mike tried to use chopsticks on his spicy peanut chicken. But all he did was drop globs of food on the table and his lap. He finally gave up and ate with a fork. During dinner, Mr. Hopkins told Kate and Mike more Dodger history.

At the end of the meal, Mike pushed his plate away. "That was really good," he said. "Now I feel like a nap." He put his head down on the table and pretended to snore.

"I didn't know how hungry I was," Kate said, yawning. "Or sleepy. I guess it's later than I thought, since we're three hours behind New York time."

"We should head home, then," Kate's dad said. He asked for the check. The waiter delivered it with three fortune cookies. Right away, Mike and Kate tore off the clear wrappers.

Mike snapped his cookie in half. He pulled

out the ribbon of thin white paper. *"Plan for excitement ahead,"* he read. "Wowee! This should be a good week."

Kate smiled, broke open her cookie, and pulled out her fortune. "Wait, mine's better," she said. *"Something lost will be found.* That has to mean we'll find my notebook! Dad, what does yours say?"

Kate's father unwrapped his fortune cookie and bit off one end. With a show, he unfolded the paper inside.

But instead of reading it out loud, he just stared at it. Mike nudged Kate. "Ummm, what does it say, Dad?" Kate asked.

"Never mind," he said, crumpling it up. "It's time to go now." He reached for his jacket.

"Oh, come on, Dad," Kate teased. "Tell us!"

Mr. Hopkins paused, and then his face

broke out into a large smile. "These things are silly," he said. He picked up the crumpled fortune and handed it to Kate.

"Watch out for strangers!" she read, her eyes wide.

"It's a mystery!" Mike said. "That's two things we have to keep an eye out for. Kate's notebook and strangers. Cool!"

Bzzzz. Bzzzz. Mr. Hopkins's cell phone rang.

"Hang on for a minute," Mr. Hopkins said. "I have to get this. It might be a work call." He put the phone up to his ear and left the table. Mike and Kate crunched on their cookies.

"It sure sounds like someone's following my dad!" Kate said. "I think we should help him keep an eye out for strangers."

Mr. Hopkins returned to the table. His face was pale.

"Dad, what's the matter?" Kate asked. "Is everything okay?"

Kate's father slumped down into his seat. "I think my fortune cookie came true," he said. "Someone just warned me to leave my job with the Dodgers. Or else there will be trouble!"

The Beach

The warm April sun woke Mike up before the alarm clock went off. He caught the smell of bacon and heard the murmur of voices coming from the kitchen. Mike rubbed his eyes and looked for Kate. The top bunk was empty. She must have gotten up even earlier.

"Hey, look who's finally awake!" Kate said as Mike came out from Mr. Hopkins's guest bedroom. "Just couldn't keep away from the pancakes, eh?"

Mike sat down at the table. Mr. Hopkins placed a large plate of steaming pancakes in front of him. Mike poured himself a glass of orange juice and picked two pieces of bacon from a plate in the middle of the table. Kate was already halfway through her breakfast.

"Guess what Dad gave me," Kate said. She held out a small black notebook. It was just like the one her father carried in his shirt pocket. "This is to replace the notebook I lost in the airport. I've already written down some of the things I want to see. We're going to start with Dodger Stadium, right after breakfast."

"Cool!" Mike said in between gulps of orange juice. "Hey, Uncle Steve, did you figure out who called you last night at the restaurant?"

"No. After you kids went to bed, I talked with the team's manager," Mr. Hopkins said.

"He called the police. Dodgers security was also notified."

"Who do you think is after you?" Mike asked.

"I don't know, but whoever it is also stole a cell phone from our hitting coach yesterday," Mr. Hopkins said. "Maybe it's a San Francisco Giants fan, trying to cause some trouble. The Dodgers and the Giants have been huge rivals since both teams moved out here in 1958. Giants fans are mad we beat them last year, so maybe they're looking for revenge."

Mike nodded and finished off his pancakes. While Kate's father cleaned up the dishes, Kate and Mike found their hats and filled water bottles for their day of sightseeing. On the way out, Mike grabbed a baseball from his luggage and put it in his sweatshirt pocket.

They started sightseeing across the street
at Palisades Park. The park was a long ribbon of green grass nestled between the main
street and a cliff overlooking the Pacific
Ocean. Joggers ran by. Palm trees rustled in
the morning breeze.

"This is pretty," Kate said. She pulled out
her camera and took a picture of the beach.

"Look! A Ferris wheel!" She pointed to a wooden boardwalk that jutted out into the ocean.

"That's the Santa Monica Pier," her father said. "We can go down there another time."

Kate snapped some more pictures of the ocean, the pier, and the palm trees. Then Mr. Hopkins went to get the car out of the garage.

"Are you on the lookout for strange people?" Mike asked Kate while they sat on the grass under a palm tree. "Maybe we can figure out who's following Uncle Steve and why."

When Mr. Hopkins pulled up, the kids hopped in the car, and they drove to Dodger Stadium.

They arrived just in time for the ten o'clock tour. It started on the concrete deck at the top of the stadium. Below the deck were rows of empty seats. Mike, Kate, and Mr.

Hopkins wore baseball hats to shield their eyes from the bright California sun. The tour guide, a tall, thin man in a Dodgers baseball cap, stepped out of a nearby elevator.

"Hello, everyone," he said as he collected tickets. "My name is Dan. Welcome to the beach!" Dan swung his outstretched arm across the view of the stadium behind him.

"Uh, Dan?" Mike piped up. "We're not at the beach. We're at Dodger Stadium." The other fans in the tour group nodded.

Dan smiled. "That's what you think!" he said. "Take a closer look at the colors of the seats in the stadium. The lowest section of seats is yellow. The next section up is gold. The section above that is light blue. And, finally, these seats near us at the top are dark blue. Anyone know why?"

Everyone looked at the seats in the different

levels of the stadium. "Maybe it was cheaper to buy different-color seats," a woman in a Yankees shirt joked.

"No, I'll tell you why," Dan said. "Remember, the Dodgers built this stadium when they moved to California from New York. They wanted the stadium to remind people of a California beach. The yellow seats are the sun. The gold seats are the sand. The light blue ones are the color of shallow water. And the dark blue seats are the deep blue sea or the sky."

"That's so cool!" Mike said.

"That's not all," Dan added. "See the pavilion seats in the outfield?" Everyone nodded. "Look at the roof of those seats. What shape is it?"

"It's wavy," said a man in a cowboy hat.

"Exactly," Dan said. "It's like waves

33

crashing on the beach! What could be more California than that? Come on. Let's take a look at the rest of the stadium."

Dan led the group through the ballpark. Along the way, he told them that Dodger Stadium was the third-oldest major-league ballpark. Only Fenway Park in Boston and Wrigley Field in Chicago were older.

One of the first stops on the tour was the pressroom. Everyone took a seat at the rows of long desks. In front of them were large, open windows that overlooked home plate. Behind them was a private dining room for the sports reporters. Dan pointed out the free ice cream machine in the corner.

"Wow! No wonder your mom likes being a reporter!" Mike whispered to Kate.

After spending fifteen minutes telling them about Dodger history, Dan led the tour group to the Dugout Club. The Dugout Club was a special restaurant under the seats behind home plate. It also had trophy cases with signed bats, a home plate from Ebbets Field in Brooklyn, World Series trophies, and other special items.

The group fanned out across the room. Mike and Kate admired the trophies and cases of valuable souvenirs. Then they walked over to the far wall. It was covered with pictures of famous Dodgers.

"Hey—what's Babe Ruth doing in a Dodgers uniform?" Mike asked. He pointed to a framed photograph halfway up the wall. It showed Babe Ruth in a Dodgers shirt and a cap with a *B* on it. "I thought he only played for the Red Sox and the Yankees!"

"He also played one season for the Boston Braves, at the end of his career," Dan said.

"But he always wanted to be a manager. The Brooklyn Dodgers hired him as a first-base coach in 1938. He only coached for one summer."

Dan led them up to the Dodgers dugout, on the third-base side of the field. They weren't allowed on the infield grass, but Dan said they could explore the dugout. Mike and Kate scrambled over to the players' benches and took pictures. Mike snapped a picture of Kate picking up the telephone that hung on the wall and pretending to call the bull pen for a new pitcher.

When the tour ended, Dan led the group back to the top deck. Mike, Kate, and Mr. Hopkins stayed behind. Mr. Hopkins wanted to talk with one of the Dodgers' coaches. He had spotted the coach over by first base.

"You kids wait here while I talk with

Tommy," Mr. Hopkins said. "Then we'll do some more sightseeing."

Mike and Kate waited by the infield railing. They pretended to manage a game and make baseball signs for imaginary hitters. Kate's first batter hit a line drive double. Mike's batter had three balls and two strikes before he hit a ball high into the left-field stands. Mike followed the imaginary ball with his eyes. It flew into the upper deck of the stadium. "Home run!" Mike yelled as he pumped his fist. "Yeah!"

As he watched the ball, something caught his attention. "Hey, what's that?" Mike asked Kate. He pointed to a man near the dark blue seats at the top of the stadium. The man wore a white polo shirt, tan pants, and a blue Boston Red Sox baseball cap. A black backpack hung over his shoulder, and he held a pair of binoculars up to his eyes. The binoculars were directed toward Mr. Hopkins and the Dodgers coach.

Kate gasped. "He's spying on my father!" she said. "Maybe he's the one who called last night!"

"Quick, follow him," Mike said. "Before he gets away!"

Pictures of
a Stranger

Kate and Mike tore up the concrete stairs to the main concourse. They ran to the elevator they had taken earlier with the tour group. Mike pushed the white UP button and waited. Nothing happened. He pushed it again. Still nothing.

"It's not even lighting up," Kate said, pacing near the elevator door. She pointed to the small metal lock below the elevator button. "I think you need a key to open it."

Mike gave Kate's elbow a tug. "Come on, let's look for the stairs," he said. Down the hall, they found a stairway. Mike and Kate hustled up the stairs until they came to the next level.

Mike took off to the right, on the third-base side. He was halfway down the hall when he heard Kate call out, "Wait! We're on the wrong floor!"

Mike stopped and turned around. Kate was pointing to the rows of seats on their right side. "Look at the color of those seats. They're light blue. We need to go up another level to the dark blue seats!"

They took the steps two at a time until they reached the top level. They shot out of the stairway and along the top deck of the stadium to the aisle where they had seen the man.

Kate skidded to a stop. "He's gone!" she panted. Mike pulled up right next to her. He

looked down the aisle to the railing overlooking the field. All the seats were empty. No one
was standing in the aisle. The man with the
binoculars had vanished.

"We missed him," Kate said. She stamped
her foot on the concrete step. "Drat! I thought
we had him. Let's get down to the field before

my father notices we're gone. Don't say anything about this to him. I don't want him to worry."

Mike and Kate made it back to the dugout just as Kate's dad and Tommy were finishing their conversation.

"There you two are," Mr. Hopkins said. "What do you say we do some sightseeing? I know a good place to start—Hollywood."

Kate and Mike exchanged a glance. Obviously her father hadn't noticed the man with the binoculars.

"That sounds great," Kate said. "Hollywood. We can look for movie stars."

After leaving the ballpark, they drove for about twenty minutes to Hollywood Boulevard. Mr. Hopkins parked the car on the street, and they walked to Grauman's Chinese Theatre.

The building was shaped like a large Chinese pagoda. "What's so special about Grauman's?" Mike asked. "Do they show only Chinese films or something?"

"Maybe if you had read my *guidebook* instead of that *baseball* book, you'd know," Kate said with a smile. "It's actually just a movie theater from the 1920s. They built it in a Chinese style to make it seem special. But what's really important is the sidewalk. Look."

Kate pointed to the ground. Underneath their feet were slabs of gray cement.

Mike wasn't sure what he was supposed to see. And then he noticed handprints and footprints pressed into the cement. All around them were names scrawled in concrete.

"There's Darth Vader from *Star Wars*," Mike cried. "And Donald Duck!"

Soon, Mike and Kate were both running around the courtyard, reading off the names of famous movie stars. Kate took pictures of Mike placing his hands into the handprints of Tom Hanks. Mike took pictures of Kate testing her shoe size against Julie Andrews's footprints. Then he took a picture of Kate and her father in front of the theater.

After they had checked out all the prints, Mr. Hopkins drove them to nearby Griffith Park.

"There's a hiking trail that leads up to the Griffith Park Observatory," he said as they got out of the car. "At night you can see the planets through the observatory's telescope. But during the day it has a great view of L.A."

Leaving the parking lot, Mike, Kate, and Mr. Hopkins hiked across a small stream and followed a dirt trail uphill. The trail wound past trees, rocks, and picnic areas.

"Okay, kids, I've got a riddle about the Dodgers," Mr. Hopkins said while they walked. "What's something that only the Dodgers once had, but now all major-league teams have, too?"

"The dugout!" Mike shouted.

"No, not quite," Kate's dad replied.

Kate loved trivia questions. She bit her lip and tried to recall the ballpark tour that morning.

Mike pulled the baseball from his sweatshirt pocket. He tossed it in the air with his right hand while he thought. Then he remembered seeing retired numbers under the roof of the outfield seats.

"Forty-two!" Mike shouted.

"What?" Kate said. "Forty-two?"

Mr. Hopkins smiled. "That's right, Mike! You got it. Number forty-two was Jackie Robinson's number. He was the first African American player in the major leagues. He played for the Brooklyn Dodgers starting in 1947. The Dodgers retired his number in 1972. In 1997, all the other major-league teams retired it, too, to honor him."

"Shoot," said Kate, who hated to lose any competition. She kicked a small stone off the path. "That wasn't fair. Mike read that entire book about the Dodgers."

"But you took the tour this morning," Mr. Hopkins said. "The guide talked about Jackie Robinson and number forty-two, so you knew the answer as well. Mike was just faster."

"Well, let's do another question," Kate insisted. "Double or nothing, Mike!"

"Not right now," Mr. Hopkins said. "Maybe we can have round two another time."

About halfway up, the trail to the observatory split. To the left was a steep, rocky shortcut that wound through some scrubs. To the right was a smoother, easier trail. Taking the lead to prove she could beat Mike, Kate scrambled up the steep trail. Mike made it up a minute later, huffing and puffing. Kate's father followed. All three stopped at the top to catch their breath. Kate was about to pull out her camera and take a picture when she heard rocks go tumbling down the trail.

"What was that?" Mike asked.

"I don't know," Kate's father said. "I don't see anyone."

"It could be a mountain lion," Kate said. "I read about them in the guidebook. There are loads of them in the hills around L.A.!"

"Mountain lions?" Mike asked. "Here?" He bared his teeth and snarled at Kate. Then he reached out and made a pawing motion at her. *"Rrrrrrrrrrr . . ."*

Kate swatted him away. "Oh, stop kidding around," she said.

Another short hike took them to the green grass in front of the Griffith Observatory. From there they could see the craggy green and brown folds of the Hollywood Hills.

"There's the famous Hollywood sign!" Kate called out. She pointed to the left. Large white letters, as tall as a house, stood on the hill. They spelled *HOLLYWOOD.*

Mike took a picture of Kate and her father, with the sign in the background. Then he hung out on the grass while Kate took a few more pictures. Her father went to get a drink from the water fountain near the snack bar.

Kate flopped down on the grass next to Mike. She turned over her digital camera and started reviewing the pictures they'd taken that day.

After a minute, she nudged Mike. "You'll never believe this," she said. "That man we saw this morning with the binoculars is in a bunch of our pictures!"

The Dodger

Mike leaned over to study Kate's pictures.

"Look in the back, behind the palm tree," Kate said, showing Mike a picture from the park that morning. "See the man in the blue baseball cap? The guy turning sideways? It looks like he's trying to hide his face!"

Kate went to a shot from Grauman's Chinese Theatre. It was a photo of Mike. But behind him was a man in a white shirt bending down.

Kate pushed the forward button on the camera again. She came to a picture that Mike had taken just a few minutes ago. The picture showed Kate and her father with the Hollywood sign. In the background, Mike could see a figure dressed in tan pants, a white shirt, and a blue baseball cap. He was ducking out of the picture.

"Hey! We saw him at the airport, too, remember?" Mike said.

"You're right, when we were looking for movie stars!" Kate said. "That was just before my notebook was stolen. I'll bet he took it!"

"He sure looks suspicious. He's always trying to dodge out of the picture," Mike said.

"Dodging out of the way. Ha! That's it! He's the L.A. Dodger!" Kate cried. "I bet he's the one causing problems for my dad. Maybe he's still here."

Mike and Kate looked around for the Dodger. Families picnicked on the grass. Couples walked toward the parking lot. But there was no sign of a man in a white shirt and tan pants.

"I don't see him," Kate said. "He must be here somewhere, though. He's been following us all day."

"What do you think he wants?" Mike asked.

"It's got to be Dad's scouting notebook," Kate said. "The Dodger must be trying to hurt the team for some reason. He probably stole the notebooks and cell phone from the coaches. And he told my father to leave his job. Without my dad, the Dodgers might not be able to sign any good new players."

Mike put his finger up to his lips. Kate's dad was returning. Mike and Kate jumped up and headed back to the car with Mr. Hopkins.

Along the trail to the car, Kate and Mike looked for signs of the L.A. Dodger. But they didn't see any. On the way back to Mr. Hopkins's apartment, Mike stared out the back window. He was hoping to spot a car following them. But again, he saw nothing.

The sun was going down when they pulled into the garage at Mr. Hopkins's apartment. A cool breeze blew in from the ocean.

They ate dinner at a restaurant named Big Steaks. It had an outdoor patio with a colorful awning and lots of flowers.

"I feel like the Dodger is watching us," Mike whispered to Kate halfway through dinner.

"I know, but I don't see him anywhere," Kate replied. "Maybe he's taking some time off to eat, too!"

After dinner, Kate, Mike, and Kate's dad walked to the pier to try the rides.

The lights were just coming on when they reached the bumper cars. Mike handed the attendant their ride tickets and scrambled into car number three. Kate grabbed car number seven and buckled herself in.

The buzzer sounded, and the ride started. Kate rammed her car straight into Mike's. A sharp metallic smell filled the air. Small sparks flew from the top of the power poles at the back of the cars as Kate and Mike chased each other around the oval course. Mike had just chased Kate down when the cars slid to a stop.

"Not fast enough to catch up to me, are you?" Kate taunted Mike. She jumped out of her car and ran back to her father. Just as Mike reached them, a flash of pink caught his eye.

"Cotton candy!" Mike cried. He pointed to a small stand on the other side of the pier. "Can I have some? I saved room for dessert."

"You *always* save room for dessert," Kate said.

"Sure," said Mr. Hopkins. They walked over to the stand. Mike and Kate each took a soft white paper cone piled high with the sticky, sugary candy. In no time, Mike's mouth was flecked with gooey strands. Kate was pulling off clouds of the pink candy and neatly popping them in her mouth. She scanned the crowds for the Dodger but didn't see him.

"Thanks, Dad!" Kate said as they headed to the apartment. "That was a really fun day." Now that the sun was gone, the night was getting cooler. Kate was happy to be going back to the warmth of her father's apartment.

Once they reached the apartment building, Mike opened the door and bounded up the stairs to the second floor. He turned right and raced down the hall toward Mr. Hopkins's apartment.

But he stopped a few feet before he reached it. "Guys! Come quick!" he called. Kate and her dad had just stepped out of the stairway. They jogged down the hallway to Mike.

The door to Mr. Hopkins's apartment was wide open!

"You kids wait here," Mr. Hopkins said. "I'll go in and check it out." He disappeared into the apartment. Mike and Kate waited outside.

Kate leaned over to look at the door frame. "See those scratches around the doorknob?" she asked. "I'll bet the Dodger forced the door open with a screwdriver or crowbar or something. That's why we didn't see him at the restaurant or pier. He must have known we'd be at dinner and broke in!"

"Everything's safe. You can come in," Kate's father called.

Mike and Kate went into the apartment. Mr. Hopkins was standing in the middle of the living room. Mike could see that the stuff on his desk had been moved around.

"Nothing's stolen, but they did go through all my papers," Mr. Hopkins said. He brushed his hair back from his forehead and mopped his brow with the back of his hand. Then he pulled the small notebook from his shirt pocket. "Luckily, they didn't get this. If it were stolen, I might lose my job!"

A Sticky Trap

The next day, Kate and Mike slept late. At breakfast, there was no talk of the Dodger or the police. Mr. Hopkins seemed to have forgotten the previous night's break-in. Kate tried to keep her father's mind off it by asking a lot of questions about the Dodgers.

After breakfast, Mr. Hopkins locked the door securely. They had tickets for that afternoon's game at Dodger Stadium, but Mr. Hopkins had planned a surprise stop.

As they drove through L.A., Mike watched the palm trees, taco stands, and car washes roll by. California looked very different from New York.

"We're getting close," said Mr. Hopkins. "Want a hint to where we're going?"

"Yeah!" Kate said. She liked to know what was going on.

"This is easy," Mr. Hopkins said. "Unless you haven't been practicing your Spanish. Try these hints. *Negra. Brea.*"

Kate bit her lip and twirled her ponytail around her finger. "Hmmmm . . . *negra* means *black*," she said. "I think I've heard *brea* before, but I can't remember what it means."

Mr. Hopkins turned the car into a parking lot. On the other side was a large building. Next to it was a park with grass and trees. Heat simmered off the black parking area.

"Tar!" said Kate. "*Brea* means *tar* in Spanish, right, Dad?"

Mr. Hopkins nodded. "That's right. Know where we are?"

"The La Brea Tar Pits!" Mike piped up.

Kate punched Mike's leg. "Hey, no fair! How did you know?"

Mike pointed out his window to a big sign. "It says it right there," he said. "You don't always need to know Spanish. Sometimes you just have to be able to read!"

"Exactly," Mr. Hopkins said. "The La Brea Tar Pits are a bunch of pools of black sticky tar. Tens of thousands of years ago, animals got caught in the tar and died. Now you can see their remains in this museum. I thought we'd have time for a quick look before the game."

Mike jumped out of the car before Kate could punch him a second time. For the next hour, Mike, Kate, and Mr. Hopkins explored the museum. They saw tar-covered bones of saber-toothed cats, wolves, and huge mammoths. They also visited Pit 91 in the nearby park, where black bubbles popped up from pools of slimy tar.

Kate could have stayed for another hour, but it was time to leave for Dodger Stadium. Mike, Kate, and Mr. Hopkins had lunch in the car and arrived at the stadium half an hour before game time. After showing their tickets, they made their way to a section right behind home plate.

"Wow! These are great seats," Mike said. "Thanks, Uncle Steve." He sat down in the bright yellow seat next to Kate and scanned the field for players. But batting practice had ended a short while before. The players were in the locker room getting ready.

Mr. Hopkins took out a program. Before he started reading, he checked his pocket again to make sure the notebook was safe. It was.

All around them, fans filed into their seats. Most wore blue Los Angeles Dodgers hats or T-shirts. But there were also a few people with San Diego Padres hats, since the Dodgers were playing the Padres. Kate was wearing her school baseball hat. It had a big white *C* on it for *Cooperstown.*

"Psssst . . ." Mike felt something nudge his leg. It was Kate. "Keep an eye out for the Dodger. He's got to be here somewhere," she reminded him.

Mike and Kate spent a few minutes searching for a man with a white shirt and a blue Boston Red Sox baseball cap. Neither of them spotted the Dodger.

The loudspeaker crackled to life. "It's time for Dodger baseball!" The fans roared. Mike and Kate stood up and cheered as the players took the field. The Dodgers pitcher quickly struck out the first San Diego batter.

In between batters, Mr. Hopkins told Kate and Mike all about the players and their skills. As a baseball scout, he knew which players were strong hitters, which were good fielders, and which could run really fast.

The first two innings flew by. The Dodgers had runners on first and third bases with one out in the second inning. But the Padres pitcher struck out the next two batters and the inning ended. Nobody scored in the third. It was still 0–0.

Kate and Mike kept looking for the Dodger. After the third inning, Mike finally spotted something. He elbowed Kate.

"What?" Kate whispered. "Do you see him?"

"No. But I see a sign for Dodger Dogs!" Mike said. He pointed to the main concourse. "I'm hungry."

Kate rolled her eyes. "Oh, come on, they're just like any other ballpark hot dogs."

"That means they'll be good!" Mike said. He stood up. "Let's go!"

"Okay," Kate said. "But let's try not to miss too much of the game." Her dad gave them some money, and they started up the stairs toward the snack stands.

After a few steps, Mike stopped suddenly. Kate plowed straight into his back, and he almost lost his balance.

"Hey! Watch out!" Kate said.

Mike blushed. "Sorry," he mumbled. Then he lowered his head and said in a whisper, "Follow me. But don't act suspicious. Don't look around."

With that, he walked quickly up the steps as if nothing had happened. Kate scrambled to keep up. She finally caught him at the hot dog stand. Mike had just ordered two hot dogs.

"What was that about?" she asked.

Mike's eyes opened wide. "I saw the
Dodger! He's sitting about five rows back

from us, but he's wearing a red shirt and sun-glasses today. That's why we didn't recognize him. But he still has the Boston hat and is carrying a black backpack."

Kate took a look. "You're right," she said. "He must be staking out my father. He's wait-ing for a chance to steal that notebook."

Mike leaned back and tossed his baseball in his right hand. He was thinking again.

Kate continued to watch the Dodger. "We need to come up with a plan to catch him," she said, tapping her fingers on the railing. "Any ideas?"

"I've got it!" Mike said. He tossed the base-ball to his left hand. "Your notebook looks just like your dad's, right? Maybe we can trick him into going after it. Let's wait a few innings. Then we'll come back here. You can hold out *your* notebook. The Dodger will think it's your dad's, and he'll follow us!"

"I like it," Kate said. "Then what?"

"We'll set a trap and capture him!" Mike said. "The black notebook will be our tar. He'll try to take it, but he'll be caught like a saber-toothed cat in the *brea*!"

A Winning Catch

"So how are your Dodger Dogs?" Kate's dad asked. Kate and Mike scooted down the row and sat next to him.

"Really good," Kate said.

"I finished mine already," Mike said. He wiped his mouth with the back of his hand. "Maybe it's time for another!"

Kate groaned. "Not again! Aren't you ever full?" she said.

By the end of the fifth inning, the Dodgers

had pulled ahead, 3–1. Their star batter, Jorge Valens, was at the plate with two outs and no one on base.

"Watch Valens," Mr. Hopkins said to Mike and Kate. "He's *really* speedy."

The Padres pitcher threw a mean fastball straight toward the center of the plate.

POW! The ball exploded off of Valens's bat. It arced high over the first baseman's head. The right fielder ran for the outfield wall as fast as he could, but he didn't get there in time. The ball bounced on the red dirt of the warning track and rebounded off the wall. Valens rounded first and kept going. The right fielder grabbed the ball and hurled it to second.

"Run! Run! Run!" Mr. Hopkins shouted. He beat his rolled-up program against the palm of his left hand. "You've got it!"

It wasn't even close. Valens easily made second base before the throw. The fans all around Mike and Kate stood up and cheered. Mike glanced back at the Dodger.

"He's still there," Mike whispered to Kate. "Now's a good time."

Kate nodded and jumped to her feet. She held her small black notebook up high and clapped her hand against it to make noise. The next Dodgers batter came to the plate. Kate and Mike and the rest of the crowd sat down. Kate rested the black notebook on her leg. Anyone sitting behind her would be able to see it.

Down on the field, the Padres pitcher threw strike after strike. The Dodgers batter swung hard but kept missing. Three strikes. Three outs. There would be no more runs for the Dodgers that inning. Jorge Valens trotted in

from second. A batboy tossed him his glove. Valens turned and headed out to play short-stop. It was the Padres' turn to bat again.

Mike tapped Kate's leg. "Let's go!" he said.

Kate stood up and stretched her arms out wide. She held the notebook in her right hand. When she was done stretching, she leaned over and told her father they were going for a drink. Mr. Hopkins nodded, and Mike and Kate started up the stairs to the food court.

Mike watched the Dodger out of the corner of his eye as they passed his row. The Dodger was just getting out of his seat. Mike skipped a couple of steps to catch up to Kate.

"Bingo!" Mike said. "He's right behind you! Now we can set the trap."

Kate tried not to look back. She didn't want to tip off the Dodger that they were on to him. The two made their way to the food court. The Dodger, in his red shirt and dark blue baseball cap, followed about thirty feet behind them.

"Are you sure this is a good idea?" Kate

whispered to Mike when they reached the landing.

"What could go wrong?" Mike said. "He wants that notebook. He knows we have it. We're going to leave it where he can take it. Then, when he grabs it, we yell, 'Stop, thief,' and we've got him! Case closed."

Kate bit her lip. "I hope you're right," she said.

Mike and Kate brushed past a few fans. The hot dog stand stood at a corner. One side opened to the main hallway. The other side opened to a second hallway that led to an exit.

"I was thinking," Kate said. "Maybe we should look around for a security guard, just in case."

"Good idea, but there's no time. The Dodger is coming," Mike said. He nodded at the other side of the hot dog stand. "I'll watch him from there and make sure he doesn't go down that hallway. You leave the notebook in sight. Remember, when he grabs it, yell, 'Stop, thief!' "

With that, Mike melted into the crowd. Kate stood back and pretended to study the menu. She felt her heart beating fast. The customer in front of her picked up a hot dog and moved over to put mustard and relish on it. Kate spied Mike on the other side of the stand. His baseball cap was pulled down low.

It was now or never.

Kate took a deep breath and stepped forward. When she reached the order window, she rested her hands on the wide counter around the edge of the stand. She ordered a drink and French fries and started rummaging around in her pockets for money. As she searched, Kate placed the notebook on the counter to her left.

She finally pulled out a ten-dollar bill and
passed it to the man behind the counter. After
getting the change, she stepped to the right to
wait for her food. The Dodger was standing
in line to buy food. Kate could see him staring
at the notebook.

"Here you go, miss." The man from the hot dog stand handed Kate her drink and fries. "Condiments are to your right." He pointed to the plastic bottles of ketchup and mustard on a nearby table.

Kate took her food and walked over to the table. As she did, a red blur caught her eye. She turned to look.

Seeing his chance, the Dodger had left the line and snatched Kate's notebook from the counter! He slipped the notebook inside his backpack.

Kate heard Mike shout, "Now!"

She yelled, "STOP, THIEF!"

The fans standing in line jerked their heads toward Kate. She pointed at the Dodger. "He stole my notebook! Stop him!" she said loudly. "He's a thief!"

Everyone stared at the Dodger, but nobody

moved. Mike ran up to the condiments table. Slowly the Dodger turned around. He looked bigger and meaner up close.

"Zoe! Stop playing silly games, or we'll get in trouble with security," the Dodger said to Kate. He was pretending that he knew her. "I paid good money for these tickets. You'd better not cause any more problems. Now come with me before I tell your mother what you've done!"

"W-what?" Kate stammered. What was happening? This wasn't what they had planned. Kate stared back at the Dodger and spoke up. "My name is Kate, not Zoe. You just stole *my* notebook!"

A few of the nearby fans snickered. The rest just turned around to wait for their chance to order. Kate glanced at Mike. He looked as confused as she felt. Neither of them knew what to do.

"*Now*, Zoe!" the Dodger bellowed. "Stop wasting time!" He swung his black backpack over his shoulder and started walking toward the exit.

Mike could see that nobody was even trying to stop the Dodger. Their plan wasn't working!

"We can't just let him get away!" Kate yelled to Mike.

She ran over to the Dodger and pulled hard on the top of his backpack. It slid down his arm, but he grabbed the strap roughly and tugged back. Kate held on to the other strap just as hard. The Dodger pulled her close enough for her to smell the coffee on his breath.

"Let go of the backpack, kid," the Dodger snarled. "I don't want to have to hurt you. Let go if you know what's good for you!"

"No way," Kate growled back. "That's my notebook, and I want it now."

When Mike saw Kate grab the Dodger's backpack, he ran over to help. Then he stopped and backed up. He had a better idea.

The Dodger was still trying to pull the backpack away from Kate. She tried to stamp on his foot and missed. But it distracted him enough, and she gave the backpack a hard tug. It threw the Dodger off balance.

As the Dodger tried to regain his footing, Kate reached out and unzipped the backpack. She pulled it open just as Mike dashed up to them. In his right hand was a big red plastic bottle of ketchup.

"Not so fast," Mike said, sliding to a halt.

The Dodger turned to look at Mike. "Huh? Who are you?"

"You took her notebook! Give it back!"

Mike said. He planted his feet firmly and held the ketchup bottle in front of him with both hands. Before the Dodger could answer, Mike squeezed as hard as he could.

Streams of bright red tomato ketchup arced through the air.

SPLAT! SPLAT! SPLAT!

The ketchup hit the Dodger across his face and chest. Streaks of red zigzagged back and forth like strands of red spaghetti.

"HEY! Ugh!" the Dodger yelled. "Stop it!" He tried to brush the ketchup off with his free hand.

Kate gave the backpack a hard tug. Her black notebook fell out. Then her original blue notebook fell out, too. But that wasn't all. A cascade of notebooks, cell phones, and photographs also dropped to the floor.

Kate dove for her notebooks.

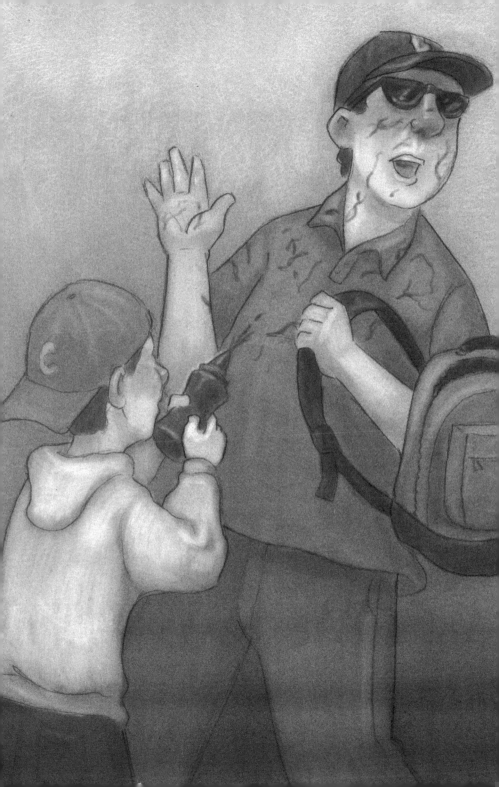

The Dodger swung around to see what happened. By now, other people had gathered around them.

"What have you kids done?" the Dodger screamed when he saw the contents of his backpack dumped on the floor. "Get away from my stuff!"

He reached down to scoop the notebooks, pictures, and cell phones into the backpack, but they slipped through his fingers. His hands were covered with ketchup. He tried to rub them clean on his shirt, but that just made everything worse.

BRRREEEEET! BRRREEEEET!

A shrill police whistle sounded. A security officer stepped into the middle of the crowd. "What's going on here?"

The Dodger glanced toward the exit and then at the contents of his backpack. He looked at Mike and Kate, and his eyes narrowed.

"Officer, I'm so glad you're here," he said loudly. "Those kids just attacked me and tried to steal my backpack. I demand you arrest them immediately!"

Mike's and Kate's jaws dropped.

The officer looked at them suspiciously. Suddenly, Kate's stomach felt sick.

"You three will have to come with me," the officer snapped. "Someone has some explaining to do."

The Real Stars
of Los Angeles

"Well, what do we have here?" Mr. Hopkins asked. He frowned at Kate and Mike. They were sitting on a bench outside the chief of security's office.

"I know you two like to look for trouble, but who'd guess you'd find it at Dodger Stadium! I never imagined you'd be brought in by security," Mr. Hopkins went on. "Everyone I work with will find out."

He shook his head. In the background, a telephone rang.

Kate slumped down on the bench. She crossed her arms and pulled her feet back under the bench. Mike shifted uncomfortably.

Kate scuffed her sneaker on the ground. Mr. Hopkins leaned over and lifted the bill of Mike's baseball cap. Then he patted Kate's knee.

"Think about it," he said. "Everyone I work with will find out that you two caught the person who's been threatening us and stealing from the team! You'll be heroes!"

"We will?" Kate asked. She sat up straight and glanced at her father. "I thought you were mad. You aren't?"

"No, of course not," Mr. Hopkins said. "I just finished talking to the chief of security. He said you outsmarted a real troublemaker!"

Mike jumped up from the bench. "All
right! I knew it would work!" he said to Kate.
"Put it there!" He gave Kate a high five.

Kate smiled. "It wasn't what we planned,
but it did work out," she said. "I guess you
caught him red-handed, Mike! Get it? With
the ketchup!"

Kate's father groaned. "Oh, that's bad. But I'm glad you made a big scene so that the security guard came over," he admitted. "How about putting that *salsa de tomate* to an even better use? Like on French fries? Mr. Thomas, the chief of security, told me he'd meet us at the Dugout Club when he was done investigating."

"Oh boy, food!" Mike called out. "Now, that's a reward!"

Mr. Hopkins led them to the Dugout Club. Mike, Kate, and Mr. Hopkins slid into a booth and watched the rest of the game on the large TVs sprinkled around the indoor restaurant. There was only one inning left. When it was over, the Dodgers had won 4–1.

A black-and-white picture was mounted on the wall of their booth. It showed two old-time Dodgers players fooling around during spring training.

At first Kate didn't notice anything unusual. But then something jumped out at her. "Mike, look at the baseball hats in that photo," she said.

Mike examined the hats. They were a dark color and had a large, fancy white *B* on the front. "That's the same *B* that's on the Boston

Red Sox's hat," he said. "But their shirts say *Dodgers.*"

"That's right, Mike," Kate's father said. "Those are the old uniforms. The *B* on the hat is for Brooklyn, not Boston. The Dodgers changed the hats after they moved to Los Angeles."

Mr. Thomas, the Dodgers chief of security, sat down across from Mr. Hopkins. He nodded to Mike and Kate.

"Hello again," Mr. Thomas said. He looked at the table covered with dishes and soda cups. "I'm glad you were able to find something to eat."

"Yup. The fries were great. Thanks," Kate said. She pointed to the black-and-white picture on the wall. "We thought the Dodger was wearing a Boston Red Sox hat, but it was a *Brooklyn* hat!"

"That's pretty good detective work," Mr. Thomas said. "Your Dodger's real name is Zoot Tambor. He is a private detective from Brooklyn. A rich woman hired him to scare the team. She loved the Dodgers when she was little, and she wants them back in Brooklyn. She was hoping after all the problems that they would leave L.A."

Mr. Hopkins slapped the table. "So that's why he was trying to get my scouting notebook!" he said. "And why he made those threatening calls. How did he steal the cell phone and the other items from the coaches and managers?"

Mr. Thomas shifted in his seat and straightened his tie. "Well, um, that was a mistake," he admitted. "He got a job with the cleaning crew and had access to the locker rooms and offices. We'll make sure that doesn't happen again."

"What's going to happen to him?" Kate asked.

"We've called the police," Mr. Thomas said. "They're going to question the woman from Brooklyn, too. Zoot Tambor has already been arrested. The police will decide what to charge him with later. But I can tell you, he won't be getting close to the L.A. Dodgers anytime soon! Now we can get back to baseball and winning some games."

Mr. Hopkins snapped his fingers. "That reminds me," he said. He reached into his shirt pocket and pulled out *his* notebook. "I've got some notes on a few players who would be great for the team. Looks like it's safe to give them to the manager. I'll do that on our way out."

Mr. Thomas stood up. "I've got to get back to my office," he said. "As our thanks for catching the Dodger, we want you to come to tomorrow night's game as our guest. Make sure to come early, because we have a special job for you."

"A special job?" Mike asked. "Like helping the batboy?"

"Not exactly, but you will help the team," Mr. Thomas told them. "We'd like you to go up to the broadcast booth and meet Vern Samson, our announcer. He's pretty famous around here. And while you're there, you two can start the game by announcing, 'It's time for Dodger baseball!' over the loud-speakers!"

Mike's eyes opened wide. "Wow!" he said. "It's like we'll be in charge of the baseball game. Maybe we can say it's free Dodger Dog day or something!"

"Not so fast, Mike," Mr. Hopkins said. "It's

a pretty big honor just to introduce the game."

"Okay," Mike said. "But you can't blame me for trying."

Mr. Thomas laughed. "See you tomorrow night," he said.

"I have one last thing to show you," Mr. Hopkins said as they left the restaurant. They rode the elevator up to the top level of the stadium. It was twilight, and the moon was just coming out. The stadium was empty except for the cleaning crew picking up the trash from the day's game. The mountains behind center field were mostly dark, though Mike and Kate could still make out the large THINK BLUE sign on one of the hills. Just over the mountains, the stars were starting to twinkle.

"Isn't it wonderful up here at night?"

Kate's father said. "It's so peaceful and quiet, it's hard to believe you're in the middle of a big city."

"It was fun looking for movie stars in Hollywood yesterday. But they're just movie stars. It's nice to see the stars up in the sky at night," Kate said.

"You're right, Kate," her father said. "But by capturing the Dodger, I'd have to say that today, you and Mike were the *real* stars of Los Angeles."

Dugout Notes
☆ Dodger Stadium ☆

Vern Samson. Vern Samson doesn't exist. But Vin Scully does. He is the most famous Dodger who wasn't a baseball player. For over sixty years, Scully was the play-by-play announcer for the Dodgers. He started broadcasting Brooklyn Dodger games in 1950. Scully continued for many, many years after the team moved to Los Angeles. He was famous for saying, "It's time for Dodger baseball!" at the start of each game.

Jackie Robinson. Jackie Robinson made history as the first African American to play in the major leagues. The Brooklyn Dodgers hired Robinson in 1947. Although Robinson had to endure harsh racial prejudice, he always played with dignity and control. He was the second baseman for the Dodgers for ten years and played in six World Series. He retired before the team moved to California.

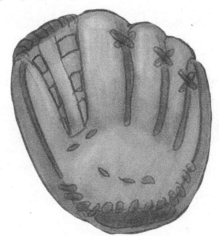

Ebbets Field, Brooklyn. Ebbets Field in Brooklyn was the home of the Dodgers from 1913 until 1957. After that, they moved to California. Ebbets Field was small and cramped, which some people felt made the games even more exciting.

Dodger Dogs. Most baseball fans like hot dogs. But Dodger fans love Dodger Dogs. At Dodger Stadium, Dodger Dogs can be cooked two ways, either steamed or grilled. Many people think that to be real Dodger Dogs, the hot dogs need to be grilled. Dodger fans started calling their hot dogs Dodger Dogs around the time the team moved to California.

Dodger Stadium. Dodger Stadium is the largest major-league ballpark. It sits on top of a hill in Elysian Park in central Los Angeles. The Dodgers have played there since 1962, when it opened. From 1958 to 1961 they played at the Los Angeles Memorial Coliseum. Dodger Stadium is so big that it even has its own zip code!

The San Francisco Giants. The San Francisco Giants is the team that Dodgers fans love to hate. The Giants moved from New York City to California the same year that the Dodgers did. They've been fierce rivals ever since.

The Hollywood sign. The Hollywood sign is high up on the side of the hills outside of Los Angeles. Fans can see the sign from the top deck of Dodger Stadium. The large white letters spell out HOLLYWOOD. Each letter is forty-five feet tall. That's taller than most houses!

Think Blue. The Dodgers have a smaller (but still large) sign on top of a hill just outside of Dodger Stadium. It reads THINK BLUE in large blue letters. Blue is the Dodgers team color.

First high five. Some people believe that two Dodger players gave each other the first high five in 1977. Other people say it was invented by a basketball player in the 1960s. Either way, it's still one of the best ways to celebrate a sports victory!

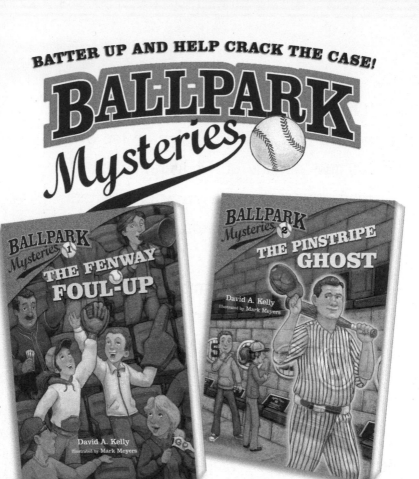

BATTER UP AND HELP CRACK THE CASE!

BALLPARK Mysteries

BALLPARK Mysteries 1
THE FENWAY FOUL-UP
David A. Kelly
Illustrated by Mark Meyers

BALLPARK Mysteries 2
THE PINSTRIPE GHOST
David A. Kelly
Illustrated by Mark Meyers

Each book in this brand-new mystery series is set in a different American ballpark. Fun facts about each ballpark appear at the end of the book, giving young fans the sports trivia they crave.

RHCB